# Ratboy

by

Pippa Goodhart

Illustrated by Polly Dunbar

**You do not need to read this page – just get on with the book!**

First published in 2004 in Great Britain by
Barrington Stoke Ltd, Sandeman House, Trunk's Close,
55 High Street, Edinburgh EH1 1SR



ISBN 1-842991-83-3

Printed by Polestar Wheatons Ltd

## MEET THE AUTHOR – PIPPA GOODHART

*What is your favourite animal?*
A cog (a cross between a cat and a dog)
*What is your favourite boy's name?*
Mouse
*What is your favourite girl's name?*
Annie-Mary-Susie (my daughters)
*What is your favourite food?*
A fresh boiled egg with bread and butter
*What is your favourite music?*
Brass band music to make me weep and laugh
*What is your favourite hobby?*
Keeping chickens (I got some for my birthday)

## MEET THE ILLUSTRATOR – POLLY DUNBAR

*What is your favourite animal?*
A cat
*What is your favourite boy's name?*
Bertie
*What is your favourite girl's name?*
Sandy
*What is your favourite food?*
Chocolate
*What is your favourite music?*
The Beatles
*What is your favourite hobby?*
Drawing

To our darling daughters,
Ellie and Rosie Cheyette

With love always
Mummy and Daddy

# Contents

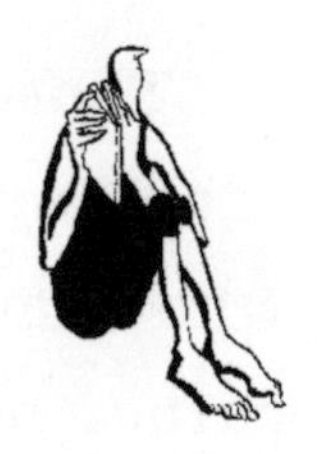

# Chapter 1
# The Best Rat

I'm the best rat in this dump. I'm not the biggest rat. I'm not the oldest rat. I'm not even the strongest rat. But I'm the fastest one, the cleverest one of the lot. Look at me. I'm sleek and lean. I'm so mean I can look after myself. Those other rats go around in gangs. They're cowards. They only feel strong when they're part of a pack. Not me. I'm strong on my own.

Those other rats don't want me with them. And I jump out and scare the children who come near the dump. Who cares? I'd rather be alone, and that's the truth. I don't have to share. I don't have to care what happens to anyone else. So when there's a sniff of something tasty arriving at the dump, I'm on to it right away while they're still thinking what to do. They know it's me who gets the best food. I let them see me sometimes, but they never catch me. I'm the best.

Shall I show you how I do it? Watch this.

My whiskers and nose twitch. I sniff. Can you smell that? Something strong and tasty, deep in that steaming, rotting rubbish. Look left and right. See? Nobody there. Softly, quickly. Scuttle. Scratch down and dig, dig, dig. Yes! I've got it! Nose it out, chomp-nibble. A chewy, rich rind of stinking, old cheese. A treat. Now, quick as a fish, back to the safety of ...

"EEeeeow!"

No! Oh! Ow! Heavy, hairy bodies, hot and smelly, are jumping on me, pushing me down into the ground. Teeth and hot breath and claws. The rat pack! Three of them. Big ones. After me and after my cheese!

# Chapter 2
# My Cheese!

I'm not giving in to that lot. They think they're better than me. I hate them. This is *my cheese* and I've still got it in my mouth. I squeal and try to shake off the teeth that are holding onto my back. I wriggle free and I run, dodging and darting. I told you that I'm good at this! I'll nip through this pipe. It's too small for their fat bodies to follow. See? I do get away.

I'll just crouch here in the box that stinks so strongly of rotten cabbage that it hides the smell of my cheese. I'll wait and those other rats will give up and go. They always do.

I stiffen stone-still in the shadows at the end of the box. I can hardly be seen. Safe. I can taste the strong cheese in my mouth. I will enjoy nibbling it when the big rats have gone. I can hear them out on the dump, poking and sniffing and searching. They are moving away now. See how easy it is to fool them?

I relax enough to begin to chew my cheesy feast. But, suddenly, the cheese is snatched from my mouth! There's another rat, a small one. It's in the box beside me! How did it get there? I squeal and turn and snarl. This small rat is in *MY* box and taking *MY* cheese! And it's making a noisy fuss that will bring those big rats back.

I nip hard into Small Rat's snaky tail and send him squealing, scuttling away. But he's got my cheese! And suddenly the big rats are back, tumbling into the box, teeth snapping.

I fight with fury and hate. And fear. Teeth and claws. Twist and struggle. Can't they see that the cheese has gone? They don't care. It's me they're after. Three big bully rats push me to the back of the box. I'm trapped. Strong teeth grab hold of my left back leg. They chomp on it and pull at it, ripping it open. Raw pain.

The rat pack go. I lie in a hot haze of throbbing pain. My leg is torn. I can't move it. I can't run or dodge any more. I lie still and wonder, *Will I ever move again?*
I shiver. Is this the end of me?

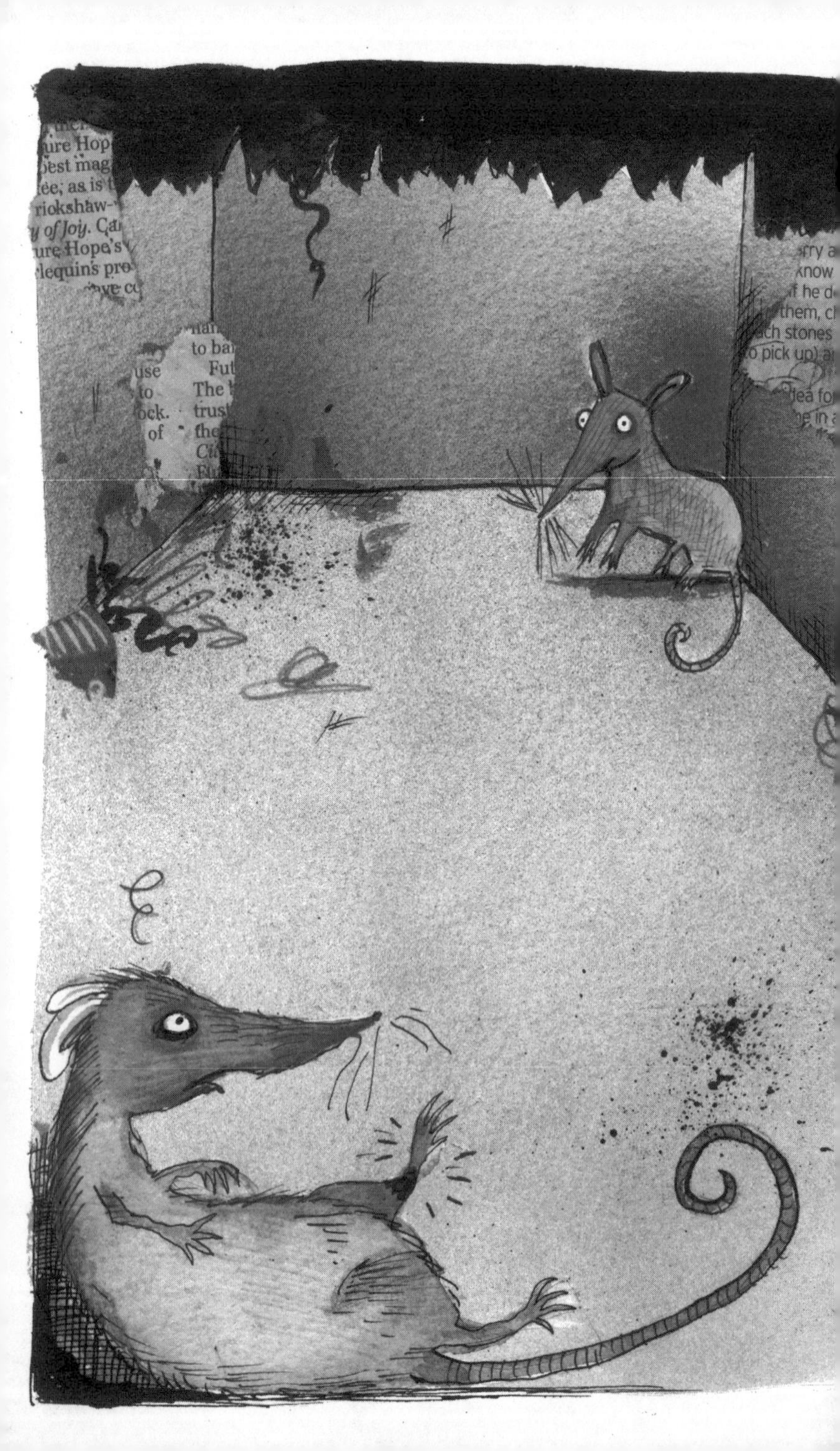

# Chapter 3
## Pain!

There's the sound of a rumbling train. It's pounding the ground all around me. It wakes me up. Pain! My head is heavy and fuzzy and faint. The rat pack! Will they come back? What will they do when they find me? My mind is fuzzy and I close my eyes. I am glad when everything goes blank.

I wake again later when the light is going dim. There's something there, warm and brown in the corner of my box. Small Rat has come back! I snarl at him, then snarl again as the pain in my leg hits me. Small Rat scuttles away. That's good.

My mouth is dry as dust. I want water. Cool, wet water. I need water.

With darkness comes the sound of rain, scampering like running feet on the top of my box.

But I can't reach it. I need to drink or I will die.

The night goes on, and the pain goes on. I cannot move.

There is a chilly smell of damp in the morning air. Oh, I must drink! My thirst is worse than the pain, and it makes me move at last. I pull my aching body off the ground and lean forward onto my front legs. Then I drag myself through the sagging, soggy box, out towards the light.

There's a small, brown puddle beside my box. I sink my nose into it and sip, sucking the water's gritty, cool wetness. My thirst slides away. Relief. I turn towards the box, but I haven't the energy to drag myself back into its safe shadows. I slump into sleep where I am.

Darkness comes and goes twice more and so does Small Rat. I feel a kind of warmth and can smell him near me. What does he want from me? I am sick and scared. I squeal at him and he goes away each time.

Alone in my fuzz of fever and pain, I lap at the puddle and let the rain cry over me, making my fur soggy and tatty.

## Chapter 4
## Food

A whiff of something prods my mind and wakes me. I sniff and twitch. I smell food. Ouch! It hurts to move. I want to slip back to hide in sleep, deep away from the pain that chews at my leg. I sniff and twitch. I need food to fill the empty hole of hunger. I must have that food. Scrabble, scamper. Ouch! My tail drags heavy behind me as I stagger towards the food smell that pulls me on. My whiskers and nose twitch and sniff, twitch and sniff. Out there, in the empty air outside the box, there's danger. But food can keep me alive. Do I want to stay alive? Not much. But I don't want to die alone in that dark, dank, rotting box with the gurgling rain laughing at my pain. I must eat.

I stagger from my box cave and sunlight slaps my face with brightness. It stops me still. But the food smell is there in the dry morning air that strokes over my fur. That breeze wakes up my mind and makes me think of something. Food and soothing stroking. I had that once, I think. I'm sure I did. Thinking of it brings more pain. Who was it that gave me food and stroked me long ago? When and where? I don't know. Maybe food will help the memory come clear.

Look, over there! A big human with a fistful of food. She's throwing it down on the ground and calling to some birds.

"Here you are, my beauties. Come and eat all you want."

Suddenly I don't care about danger. I dare to run right out onto the open ground to where the lumps of bread lie. Flapping birds fly up as I limp-run for the food.

"A rat!" The human steps back. She puts her hands to her mouth. "Go away, you horrid thing!"

I run towards the food, nose to the ground. I open my mouth and gobble and swallow and sniff-search for more. But a crumb is taken from under my nose. It's that Small Rat stealing my feast again! I reach out and bite into his strange-tasting furry neck and I shake and shake him. That food is *MINE!* The human is shouting and the birds are flapping. Small Rat runs off.

“You horrible big rat!” the woman shouts at me. “Leave the little one alone! This bread is for the birds, not for a smelly rat like you!”

I see the woman’s foot coming close and I wonder, *Will it kick me? Will she pick up a stick and hit me?* I gobble up fast all the bread that I can find. Then I scurry back to my box and I hide there, shaking and shaking. And hurting.

# Chapter 5
# Touch

The train rumbles again next day and my tummy rumbles with it. *Will that woman come again with food?* I wonder. I creep-creep out to the light and peep around me. And, yes, she's there, throwing food at the silly birds again.

Why would anybody throw away food? It must be a trap. But she hasn't caught any of the birds yet. Might she want to catch a rat like me?

There's something beyond the smell of food that pulls me to that woman, even though I fear her. I want to be close to her warm, soap-clean feet and the leather smell of her shoes again. Will she scream if she sees me? I know she won't like my snaky tail and my greasy smell of pain and drains. I know that. I know that she can never want me near her, but I still want to get close to her and her food.

The food that she is throwing today has a smell of nuts, oily-rich to crunch. Oh, I want some so much! My heart scampers like my feet and my head is whispering warnings of danger-danger, but my stomach shouts the loudest of all, *Hunger!* And suddenly I am so close to the woman's feet that I can see her neat toes in their blue-strapped sandals. The toes are bare.

These aren't the kind of feet that kick, but might they stamp down on me? I watch the foot as I snuffle up nuts.

"You again," she says, but she doesn't sound angry. "You've seen off my poor bird friends, so I suppose that you might as well enjoy the nuts, eh?" Her voice softens. "Goodness, you're a skinny thing, aren't you?"

Now I can see more than her feet. I see a plump body. An arm holds out an open hand with a nut on it. This hand isn't a fist. "Here," says the woman. "Here's a nice nut for you."

The nut is in front of my nose. My stomach tells my legs to stay but my head is shouting, "Run! Run!" But I don't run. I sniff the nut, then nibble quickly, and, oh, I want more. Her fingers touch my head and I freeze stone-stiff.

"Is that blood on your leg?" she asks. "Whatever has happened to you?"

Her fingers reach towards my bent, bad back leg. "You've been hurt."

That's when something strange happens.

As the woman touches my bad leg, I feel myself changing. My sharp nose blunts and softens. It flattens back into my face and I feel a grin growing as she moves her hand and strokes behind my ears. My body is melting into something bigger and fatter and furrier than I have ever been before. I press myself against the woman's sun-warmed legs. I begin to purr as she tickles under my chin. I have become a cat.

"There, my little rat-cat," she says.

# Chapter 6
# Beautiful Cat

I sprawl, full and floppy, along the branch of a tree. The food made me so strong that I easily clawed my way up the tree. Getting down will be hard on my poor sore back leg, but for now the leg can rest. I am safe here, high above the dump, above the rat pack and the dogs that sometimes prowl. I can loll lazily and soak the sun into my fur. I look around and see that there is nothing near except a few birds. I'm here in their tree, but the birds know that it will be my tree for as long as I choose to stay. I am strong, even though my leg is still bent and sore. I lie there and lick and lick the sore leg. That Small Rat can't come near me while I'm up here either. I smile smugly. I snooze. I close my eyes and doze and let the sun grill my fur till it's hot.

You know how a magnet has a double power? It will attract some metals, but will repel another magnet. I am like that now. I can attract the woman and make her stroke me and give me food. And I can repel Small Rat and the big rats almost as well as I could when I was a rat. I had that power to repel before, then I lost it. But the power to attract is new. It reminds me of a feeling of safety and belonging that I had long ago. I like it. I want more of it, but I'm not certain about this woman yet. I still think that she might want to trap me.

She comes and she calls for me.

"Limpy! Limpy boy?"

I lump down from the tree and amble over to her in the sunshine. Let her think that she has the power to call me to her. She hasn't really. I go where and when I like. But I'll flatter her into loving me. I will use her while it pleases me, then I'll be off and away once I'm strong again.

The woman's holding a bowl with all sorts of tasty scraps. The bowl has pictures of flowers and the food has none of the grittiness of food eaten off bare earth. I like the clean taste. I stop and sit and wash myself, leg in the air. No hurry. No worry.

"You are a very beautiful cat," she says. "Let me look at that poor leg. I'm sure that I can help it."

She scoops me into her arms, and I don't scratch. I don't want to alarm her. It is useful that she likes me. But I won't be held for long. I slip from her arms, pouring through them like water. I'd like to go back to my tree, but I wind myself around and around her warm legs to bind her to me. I'll charm her so that she likes to serve me.

"I'll see you tomorrow, Limpy," she says. That's what I want her to say. Now I go back to my tree, smug and happy, to laze and look down on the dump.

# Chapter 7
# My Lady

The woman does come back. She does what I want her to do. She brings cream to slide, cool fatty-fresh, down my throat. I purr as I lap it up slowly and smile.

"You're beautiful, cat," says the woman. She runs a finger down my furry back and I arch and purr for her.

But then I hear something that stops the purring. There's a slight scurrying, squeaking over at the rubbish dump. I stop, turn and stare. And there, in the rubbish, I can see a small, sharp face, twitching. It is a hungry face, hungry and scared. Small Rat. I know what he's after. He wants what I've got. He wants My Lady to be his lady too! He wants her to care for him.

"What is it, Limpy?" asks My Lady. "What are you staring at?"

And I know that if she sees Small Rat with his big, hungry eyes, then she will care about him too. She will love him into beauty and strength just as she has changed *me* with her kindness. But she's *MINE!*

Slick as a snake I make for the dump and I pounce, hiss-spit scratch at Small Rat.

I send him scurrying, hurrying away into the rubbish where My Lady won't see him.

Then I limp back to My Lady and flatter her with big eyes.

"Limpy," she says, "what was all that about? Who were you being fierce to?" She sounds stern and she doesn't reach down to stroke my sun-warmed coat as I want her to. So I roll on my back in the hot, grey dust and offer my fluffy chest and tummy to her touch. Then she laughs and bows down low and she strokes me and strokes me. I purr and smile. Then I twist onto my feet and lean against her legs.

"A drop more cream?" she says. I lap it up and a little bit of me loves her for it. I know that Small Rat may still be there, watching from his hiding place. I want to bind My Lady's love to me, so I push my face at her and make her stroke me again. But I worry. I can charm My Lady, but what if I leave her and Small Rat comes out and he charms her too? What if he takes my place? So today I don't leave My Lady.

She lingers for a while, talking to me, stroking me. But then she stands up tall and packs the empty bowl back in her bag.

"I must go, Limpy," she says. "I must prepare a meal for my man."

So there is another that she loves and feeds! I hate the man even though I know nothing about him. I hate him. He cannot need My Lady as much as I do!

My Lady moves away, over the open ground to the road that leads into town. I follow her, my tail thrashing angrily, but I'm worried too. I flatten my ears and keep low to the ground and hurry. I must keep sight of her. I must follow her, please her.

She must stay mine. I feel and know that the panic in me is changing me once more. What kind of creature will I become next?

# Chapter 8
# Good Dog

The roads in town are full of cars and scary. I'm afraid of them, but I must keep with My Lady or I will lose her. I am loping along, panting a little in the rising heat of midday. Panting? Yes, I have changed again. I've grown bigger and shaggier. I feel a clumsy kind of strength. My ears flap as I limp-jog along behind My Lady. I have become a dog.

"Goodness, Limpy," says My Lady when we get to her door. "Have you followed me all the way from the dump? You can't come in, you know."

So I stand still like a good dog would and I gaze up at her. I haven't really looked at her top end before. She has dark hair tied tight back so you can see all of her face. It is a round face with a big mouth and brown, worried eyes. I can see that she is kind, but she's not sure what to do about me. So I'll help her to make up her mind. I take a wobbly step towards her, limping on my bad back leg. It hurts. I whimper with pain.

"Oh dear," she says. "My poor Limpy." She bends down and hugs me.

Hear that? She said *my* poor Limpy! She owns me now and I am her dog. And I own her too. And I like that. We both own each other and nobody is going to get between us. I thump my tail and she smiles a little. She puts down her bag and she reaches a hand to pat me on the head. She asks, “Are you going to let me look at your poor leg at last? I suppose that you had better come in after all.”

I lie on the clean, cool tiles on her floor. And I hardly twitch when her fingers gently poke at my hot, heavy, dragging leg.

“Gently now, Limpy. Good boy. That’s it,” she says, all soft. “Oh, yes. I can feel your leg is broken. Now, will you trust me to mend it for you? It will hurt, but it is important to mend it well so that you can grow strong again.”

I wag my tail and I gaze up at her. I’ve got her now. She is going to care for me because of my leg. Now I’m glad of my bad leg that nearly killed me. The pain doesn’t matter because it makes My Lady love me. This bad leg will keep her busy with me, and that's good. There will be no time for her to fuss over silly birds or other rats or that man that she talked about.

But it's the man who comes to mend my leg. He smells different from My Lady, but his smell is part of the smell of this house. I can tell that he belongs here. I growl, low in my throat.

"Oh, Limpy!" My Lady scowls. She's cross with me now. So I stop growling. She comes down beside me and she strokes me and soothes me. So I let her man touch me. He moves my leg, hurting it, and he bandages it. He pushes a sharp needle into my neck and I growl low to let him know that I don't like it. But I don't snap because it is My Lady's arms that are near my mouth and I mustn't hurt her. I pant to cope with the pain and My Lady strokes and strokes. She kisses me on the head when it is over.

"You rest there now, Limpy," she tells me. "I must make some lunch."

She gets up to go into the kitchen. But I will not let her go where I cannot see her. I will not let her escape now that she is mine and I am hers. So I won't settle and rest as she told me to. I drag my leg and stagger after her, into the kitchen. She's busy, standing tall beside me and doing things with vegetables and bread and pans and cutlery. Then she sits at a table with the man. They eat and talk. I whimper a bit to make My Lady look at me. Whimper, whimper. She stops listening to the man and turns to me.

"You'll have to go out if you're going to make that horrible noise, Limpy," she says. She turns her back to me.

I don't want to make her cross. I don't want to be shut out in the yard. So I move across the floor and settle by her soap-scented feet. I lay my nose across her toes so that I will know the instant she gets up to go anywhere. And I rest at last, but I twitch in my sleep. Will she leave me or will she love me for ever?

# Chapter 9
# The Man

I spend the next days following My Lady around the house. If she stays in one room I follow her around that room with my eyes. I nose-nudge her when she spends too long talking on the telephone or reading or laughing with the man. I don't like to be ignored for long.

The nights are long when I'm down here and she's upstairs with the man. So I whine to bring her down to me. She gets cross with me but at least I know that she is there and that she knows that I'm here. Or I nose open the cupboard and go up on my newly strong back leg and steal food from the shelves. I can sleep when I'm full. Then I sleep too deep to worry.

"What a mess!" she says when she comes down in the morning. "Why do you steal when I'm giving you good meals?"

"Give him time," says the man. "It will take time for him to learn."

I begin to like the man a little.
He doesn't get cross. He smiles at me. He takes me out now that my leg is getting stronger. We go for little strolls down the street so that I can sniff and look and get to know what happens around here.

The man takes the bandage off my leg.

"How's that?" he says, and he fingers the leg gently. "I think that it has mended well."

I still limp a little, but I can run again. The man takes a ball and I go with him to the open ground. It is the open ground under the tree and near the dump. It is my old home. Is he taking me back to leave me there, back where My Lady first found me? I lag behind. I whimper.

"Come on!" he says. "What's the matter with you?"

The matter is that I'm peeping low into the hiding places all around me. Are there rats watching and waiting for the man to go so that they can get at me? I can smell them and it wrinkles my nose. A sudden feel of them being somewhere nearby makes the fur go up all along my back.

"See if you can catch this!" says the man. And suddenly there's a red ball coming through the air and bouncing off the ground. I jump and catch it and feel my old skills return. I catch the ball – woomph in my mouth – again and again, every time he throws it.

A boy called Sanjay comes along. I'd seen him before when I was a rat.

"Can I join in?" asks Sanjay.

Sanjay is fast at dribbling and kicking a ball. I have to dodge and dart to get the ball off him. It's fun. I forget about any rats. I run and jump and stop and pant, then run and jump again.

"Time to go home," says the man. He looks to me to follow him, and I do. I like this man. I don't mind sharing him with My Lady any more. I wag my tail. Sanjay walks most of the way home beside me.

"See you soon," says Sanjay as he goes into his house.

The man smiles at me and we walk to our home together. He tells me, "You know what, Limpy? We ought to give you a proper name."

# Chapter 10
# Our Boy

When we go inside, the man asks My Lady, “What do you think we should call him? Limpy is no good. He’s hardly limping at all now.”

“We could call him Laddy,” says My Lady.

“Laddy? That’s not a name. That’s just a label like Limpy,” says the man. “No, our boy needs a real name for himself.”

I'm thinking. A name that will fit after the limping is gone. "Our Boy." Are they really going to let me stay? Forever? I pant and grin and wag my tail and look from the man to My Lady and back again. What will they decide?

"I've always liked the name Marco," says My Lady. "Marco is a fine name." She crouches down and looks at me. "Would you like to be Marco?" She puts a hand on my head. Her touch does the magic again. I'm changing once more.

I rise up and stand on my back legs. I am face to face with the man and My Lady.
I open my mouth, and it's words that come out rather than a bark.

I have become a boy.

"If you like," I say. "I will be Marco."

They both smile and hug me.

Now that I'm a boy, it's even more fun when I play with Sanjay. We don't just chase a ball around now. We talk a lot, about the world and about life.

Lunchtime comes, and Sanjay is called in for dinner.

"Come, Sanjay," calls his mum. "Lunch is on the table."

"Coming," says Sanjay.

My Lady comes to our doorstep and she calls me in for lunch too.

"It's all ready, Marco. Come and wash your hands."

"Coming, My Lady," I say, and Sanjay laughs. He copies me in a silly voice.

"Coming, My Lady. It sounds as if you're her servant, Marco!"

As Sanjay runs home I wonder, *Is Sanjay right? Have I been tricked by My Lady into being her servant? Do I have to do whatever she says? No, I don't! Am I sure? I'll test it.*

"I'm not hungry," I tell My Lady when I get into the house. "I don't want your lunch."

"Really?" she says. "But it's your favourite tomato soup, Marco. And there's fresh bread and cheese and fruit. Come and eat."

I'm hungry. I like the soup that she makes.

"Oh, all right," I say. "If I have to." But I don't wash my hands. I'm not doing every single thing that she wants me to.

I'm quiet at the table. My Lady brings a bowl of soup and puts it down in front of me. It's as if she is a waitress. Maybe things are the other way around from what Sanjay thought? After all, My Lady does other jobs for me too. She washes my clothes and cleans my room.

"Are you my servant?" I ask her.

She laughs. "No I am not, Marco! Now, would you like butter on your bread?"

"But you work for me," I tell her. "That's what servants do."

"Ah," says My Lady, "I do work for you, but you don't pay me for that work, do you?"

"No," I say. "So why do you do it, then? Doesn't that make you a slave, if you work for me for no pay?"

My Lady puts down her spoon. She puts a hand on my shoulder. "No, Marco. I'm not your slave and I never will be. I work for you for no pay because I love you." She reaches up her hand and strokes my head as she used to do when I was a dog. "I love you."

# Chapter 11
# Small Rat

I think about what My Lady said. I think about it when I go out to play with Sanjay again. I think about it when I go with Sanjay into his house for a drink because it is a hot day. Sanjay has a big family. They all talk at the same time. Names fly back and forth across the room as they try to get somebody's attention.

I think about names. Some people have lots of them. The more people a person belongs to, the more names they have. I hear Sanjay's mum being called "Mum" and "Gran" and "Auntie" and "Sister". I hear her called "Margie" and "Maggie" and "Darling". I think about My Lady. The man calls My Lady "Honey". Her friends call her something else. I want her to have a name from me too.

I run out of Sanjay's house.

"Hey, where are you going?" asks Sanjay, but I'm away down the street to my house.

I find My Lady sitting at a desk doing some work. I rush to her.

"Goodness, whatever has happened?" she asks.

"My Lady," I say. "Please. Um. Would it be all right if I called you Mum?"

She smiles so big that I know the answer.

I haven't called the man anything yet, but I've got an idea for his name.

Calling her Mum has given *me* another name too. Now I'm her "son". I like that.

I could get another name if I had brothers like Sanjay has. I think I know where I might find a brother. I'd only want a little one.

"Can I have those bits of old bread?" I ask my new mum.

"Whatever for?" she asks. "Are you still hungry?"

"No," I tell her. "I just want to go and feed those birds."

"By the dump?" she asks.

"Yes," I say.

That's a lie. I'm not going to feed those silly, flappy birds at all. I'm going to see if Small Rat is still there, waiting and watching and hungry. Maybe he can turn into my new Small Brother, if I can do the magic to make him change.

Barrington Stoke would like to thank all its readers for commenting on the manuscript before publication and in particular:

Timothy Backhouse
Mrs Banham
John Bray
Joshua Brown
Bridie Carson
Ronan Collins
Steven Craddock
Lauren Endean
Yasmin Eresh
Brogan Fox
Ben Freeman
Emma Glasson
Jacqueline Hawkesford
Joseph Hill
Katherine Hudson
Jamie Johns
Jack Lindsay
Katrina Mallows
Ashley Mann
Nicola Morgand
Kristian Marshall
Mrs Alwyn Martin
Ailidh Mather
Karen McIntyre
Jade Pappin
Ella Platts
Jade Pocklington
Caroline Post
Olivia Post
Jane Rogers
Amy Stewart
Amy Toynton
Abby Tutty
Lucia Vettese
Lauren Winsley

## Become a Consultant!

Would you like to give us feedback on our titles before they are published? Contact us at the address below – we'd love to hear from you!

Barrington Stoke, Sandeman House, Trunk's Close,
55 High Street, Edinburgh EH1 1SR
Tel: 0131 557 2020 Fax: 0131 557 6060
E-mail: info@barringtonstoke.co.uk
Website: www.barringtonstoke.co.uk